Jazeera's
Journey

Also by Lisa Bruce

Jazeera in the Sun
Nani's Holiday

Lisa Bruce

Jazeera's Journey

MAMMOTH

First published in Great Britain 1993
by Methuen Children's Books Ltd
Published 1995 by Mammoth
an imprint of Reed International Books Ltd
Michelin House, 81 Fulham Road, London SW3 6RB
and Auckland, Melbourne, Singapore and Toronto

Reprinted 1996

Text copyright © 1993 Lisa Bruce
Illustrations copyright © 1993 Paul Howard

The right of Lisa Bruce to be identified as
author of this work has been asserted by him in accordance
with the Copyright, Designs and Patents Act 1988

ISBN 0 7497 1919 2

A CIP catalogue record for this title
is available from the British Library

Printed and bound in Great Britain
by Cox & Wyman Ltd, Reading, Berkshire

Contents

1. Leaving Home

The sunlight bounced off the brilliant white walls. Everything that could had gone into the shade and settled down for a rest from the heat of the day. The only movement to be seen was the rhythmic bouncing of a bright yellow ball as it patted its way along a shady verandah.

On either side of the ball stood two young girls wearing bright flowing clothes. As each girl caught and threw the ball she shouted out a name, until finally one of them faltered, missed the ball and they both collapsed in a fit of giggles. The ball rolled unnoticed along the cool tiled floor, bounced down a small flight of steps and came to rest in the corner of a flower bed, where along with a discarded sandal and a half-chewed bone it stared up at the relentless sunshine.

Panting, the two girls flopped down on a pile of cushions and sat for a while staring out at the beautiful gardens while their breathing returned to normal. Softly, one of them spoke what they had both been avoiding for so long,

'I'll miss you.'

'I know.'

There was silence as thoughts swirled around in each of their minds.

'I wish that I didn't have to go,' the taller of the two said, lowering her eyes and staring at her pretty polished nails.

'I wish that I could come with you,' the other replied, reaching out and holding her friend's hand.

There was silence again.

'Still,' the second girl said, shifting her position slightly, 'just think what an adventure it will be. All the exciting places you will see and all the new people you will meet.'

'I know,' the other replied unenthusiastically, still staring at her hands. She would miss her friend more than anything else, except perhaps her grandmother. She hated the thought of having to leave her grandmother behind.

'Ayisha! . . . Jazeera! What are you doing!'

A willowy figure holding a sleepy

little boy appeared at the door and frantically beckoned them inside.

The girls followed her into the house where the soft whirring of the electric fans sent a cool breeze over their faces. From further inside the house came the sounds of people stirring. Putting Omar on a chair, the lady smiled at them. 'Now then, Ayisha, it's time for you to go home. Jazeera must help me with the packing, there is still much to be done.'

Ayisha nodded.

'You will come and see me tomorrow though, won't you?' Jazeera asked her friend.

'But you will be leaving early in the morning and I will be at school.'

There was a soft rustle of fabric behind the girls as Jazeera's mother approached them. Sensing her daughter's disappointment she said, 'How would you like to ride with us in the car to the airport tomorrow, Ayisha? I'm sure we could squeeze you in.'

Hearing this the two girls jumped up

and down in their excitement hugging and kissing each other.

'Oh, can she really?' cried Jazeera.

'How wonderful!' exclaimed Ayisha. 'Are you sure that it will be all right?'

'Don't worry about it,' said Jazeera's mother. 'I will speak to your teacher, Mrs Khan, to see if you can miss school for a morning. Now run along, both of you.'

Ayisha dashed happily down the path and out of the gate.

Jazeera waved to her and turned slowly back towards the house. She was certainly going to miss Ayisha.

Inside she found her grandmother busy putting the last of her brother Omar's clothes in a case. Looking at her, Jazeera felt proud; her grandmother still looked young for her age, even though she did have grey hair. Her wrinkles suited her, they made her face look soft and wise. Whenever Jazeera had any problems Nani always had time to listen and a piece of advice to give.

They had such good times together. How was she going to manage without her dear old Nani to talk to . . .?

The black car slid into the parking space. One by one Jazeera's family piled out on to the baking-hot car park. Jazeera and her grandmother walked silently hand in hand towards the airport. Ayisha had come out in nasty red spots during the night and the doctor had confined her to bed for a week.

Jazeera had been very upset when she had heard the news, but there was nothing anyone could do.

Jazeera watched bright-eyed as her father checked in and their luggage trundled off down the small conveyor belt ready to be loaded on to the plane. All they had to do now was wait for their flight to be announced.

Their journey had been planned for so long that Jazeera could hardly believe that it was actually happening. As they

waited she glanced around her at the vast airport lounge. It was crowded, just like the bazaar, but this time people were milling around chatting to their relatives or lying slumped in the hard plastic chairs trying to sleep. Bright lights glared out from the ceiling and every so often a pleasant voice would announce the arrival or departure of a flight over the tannoy. Jazeera's father stood where he could keep an eye on the huge information board, which occasionally flipped over rapidly when a new flight was ready to be boarded.

Little Omar, full of excitement, raced up and down between the aisles of waiting people. Jazeera's parents chattered to her aunt and uncle reminding them to give messages to various neighbours. Jazeera and Nani sat holding hands, watching everything.

'It will soon be time for you to go, Zeeraji,' Nani said affectionately.

Jazeera gulped. All the excitement that had been mounting inside her vanished and she realised that very soon she would have to say goodbye to her Nani, perhaps for ever. A lump rose in her throat.

'I . . . I . . .' she stammered.

'Shhh . . .' soothed her grandmother. 'It's all right, you don't have to say anything.'

Jazeera looked into her grandmother's dark brown eyes. Jazeera did want to go with her family to live in the west, she had heard so many stories about how exciting life was there. And she did want to see her Aunty Rehanna, Uncle Javed and Salma Apa, the cousin she had never met. Yet at the same time she didn't want to leave Nani behind.

If only this were just a holiday, she thought. If only I were coming back in a few weeks . . .

'Flight 379 to the departure gates.' The voice on the tannoy interrupted her

thoughts. 'I repeat, Flight 379 to the departure gates.'

With a strangled sob Jazeera threw herself into her Nani's arms and buried her head in the soft folds of her starched white saree. The two of them stayed locked together until Jazeera felt an urgent tap on her shoulder.

'Come along, you must hurry up.' It was her Aunty Naseema calling to her and beckoning frantically.

At the departure gate there was much kissing, hugging and blowing of noses as everybody said goodbye to everyone else. Jazeera was squashed and mauled until, before she knew it, she was being ushered towards the passport control. Desperately she turned her head for one last look at her grandmother. There was so much that she hadn't said, so much that she had wanted to say and yet somehow there had been no need. Somehow her grandmother understood her perfectly. The slightly stooping, grey-haired figure waved to her.

'I'll write to you, Nani,' Jazeera yelled over the noise of the crowd. 'I'll write to you every day.' With that the surge of people carried her off around the corner, out of sight.

Nani stood watching her granddaughter disappear.

'Goodbye,' she whispered as she raised her hand to brush a single tear from her cheek.

Dear Nani,

I was so sorry that Ayisha was ill when we left. I wanted to say goodbye to her properly. When you see her next please tell her that I miss her very much and that I don't think that I will make friends with anyone as nice as her in this country.

We are all very tired as the flight was very long. I got a bit bored on the plane but Mummy said that I behaved myself very well, not like Omar! The naughty boy ran off with the flight attendant's hat and she had to chase him up and down the plane to get it back. Mummy was very angry with him, but I guess that he was bored too.

After he was told off Omar began to cry VERY LOUDLY, the passengers in front of us turned round and gave Mummy some very cross looks. In the end Mummy gave Omar a sweet to make him stop crying. It wasn't fair I didn't get a sweet and he was the one who was being naughty. I tried to explain this to Mummy but she wasn't in the mood to listen. I expect that she was tired too.

The plane was delayed for five hours. Poor Uncle Javed had to wait all that time at the airport for us. He was tired too. Uncle helped us into a taxi with all our bags. Honestly, Nani, I couldn't understand a word that the taxi driver spoke. Uncle said that he had a heavy accent but it sounded to me like a completely different language! I do hope that all the people here don't talk with a 'heavy accent' or I'll never manage.

We are staying in Uncle's spare room

for the moment. It is very crowded and Omar and I have to share a bed. I wish we didn't, he wriggles and fidgets all night and kicks the covers off. I can't wait until we move into our own house.

Aunty Rehanna says 'thank you' for the silks that you sent for her and Uncle was very pleased with the books. I must tell you, Nani, that the cardigan which you knitted for me is wonderful. I am wearing it all the time. It is quite cold here even though it is summertime.

Mummy only unpacked my things this morning and this is the first letter that I am writing. Tell Ayisha that I will write to her too, as soon as I can. Give Shebu a big cuddle from me and tell her that I miss her. Please don't forget to take her out for a walk every day.

Lots of love,

Jazeera

Dear Jazeera,

How lovely it was to hear from you so soon. The house seems very quiet without you and Omar around. I hardly know what to do with myself.

I have been keeping busy taking Shebu for her walks. Yesterday we went past the bazaar and we met Ayisha and her mother so I gave them your message. I think that Ayisha was as upset as you were that she couldn't come to the airport. She is much better now but the doctor has said that she can't go back to school yet. I think that Ayisha is lonely without you. She told me to send you her love.

Shebu is missing you too, but I am looking after her very well. I haven't forgotten her bone from the butcher and now that you have gone she comes and sits by my chair on the verandah in the evenings.

She is as naughty as ever though. Last week she sneaked into Uncle's chicken coop when he wasn't looking and chased all the poor chickens. There was such a tremendous uproar of clucking, screeching and squawking that the neighbours came round to see what was happening. The poor hens were in a complete frenzy running everywhere and Shebu was barking madly in her excitement. She thought that it was all good fun. Uncle was very cross and when he finally managed to get Shebu out she was covered in feathers and she looked like a chicken herself! I had to scold her thoroughly, but she ended up sneaking back to my chair and she looked at me with her melting brown eyes so I forgave her. (Your uncle still hasn't, though!)

Be a good girl and give my love to everyone. How are Aunty and Uncle and Salma? It is such a long time since I have seen your Salma Apa, she was only a little girl when Aunty Rehanna and Uncle Javed left India. Give her my love.

Love and kisses

Nani

2. A New Home

Jazeera sat staring out of her bedroom window. Below her on the shining street she saw a tiny figure scurrying along, huddled under a black umbrella. Night was falling and the person was probably in a hurry to get home. All of a sudden a gust of wind caught the umbrella and turned it inside out. The little figure was pulled helplessly along underneath it.

Jazeera had never seen weather like this before. Back in India rain was welcomed, it was refreshing. Not like this. Here the rain soaked right through your clothes and chilled your bones. Here the rain was depressing. With her breath steaming up the window,

Jazeera didn't see what happened as the figure disappeared round the corner still battling with the wind and rain.

Jazeera's gaze travelled along the row of tall narrow buildings opposite. Built with dark brick, she could hardly call them houses. They were not at all like the houses that she was used to back in India; why, Nani's house was open and spacious with no glass in the windows just shutters opening on to wide spreading gardens. Birds and animals wandered about freely and inside the house was a constant noisy bustle of preparation. Jazeera was always being called to help make ready the beds or food for the steady stream of guests.

The houses across this new damp street stared silently at each other, eyes closed tightly behind net curtains. It was as though they were annoyed at being so close together. Jazeera stared for a while at the building directly opposite. It was identical to all the others on the street, except that its door was painted blue. Jazeera had never seen the people who lived there, as if they were afraid to let anyone into their lives. That would never happen back home, no matter who you were, you were never alone.

Blowing her nose violently Jazeera sat back on her bed. She opened her letter pad and sighing dejectedly to herself she began to write . . .

Dear Nani,

It was lovely to hear from you. I am glad that you met Ayisha, I hope she gets better soon. Please send her my love when you see her again.

I am missing you SO much, Nani. It is cold and miserable here. It always seems to be raining and we can't go outside. I miss my old bedroom. I miss Uncle's chickens and I miss my darling doggy, Shebu. Oh wasn't she naughty! I laughed and laughed when I read your letter. Give her a big kiss from me. Talk to her about me so that she doesn't forget me, please.

Everyone here is getting very cross and bad tempered. We are still staying in Uncle's spare room and it is very crowded. There has been some sort of delay with our new place and Daddy spends hours talking on the phone to all sorts of people. Yesterday I heard Aunty complaining to Uncle about the phone bill, but I didn't tell Daddy.

Daddy is working at Uncle's restaurant now. It has lots and lots of red chairs in it. Omar and I played a

brilliant game of chase around the tables and chairs until Uncle told us off. He's such a spoilsport.

Most of all though, I miss you, dearest Nani. I wish that I could jump on the next plane and fly straight back to India. When I told Mummy this she got cross and said that I was a big girl now and should learn to be patient and accept things. She doesn't understand how upset I am. You are the only one who understands me.

I got very fed up this evening and I told Mummy that I didn't want to come to this horrid old house in this horrid old country. I have been sent to bed for saying that. At least it has given me some peace and quiet in the bedroom and I have been able to write to you without Omar crawling all over me.

Please write soon, I miss you all so much.

Love Jazeera

Dear Jazeera,

Oh my darlingji, I am so sorry to hear that you don't like your new home. You know, you are very lucky to be there. Travelling is such a wonderful thing to be able to do. I have never been out of India, but when I was a little girl my friends and I often used to play at 'going on a journey'. We would line up chairs like a train, I would be the driver and my friends were the passengers. We used to pretend that we were visiting exciting places like Mecca, the Nile or the Tower of London. Now you are going to have all the opportunities and be able to do all the things that I wanted to do. You are very, very fortunate.

I know that it is hard for you to leave all your friends and your life behind but we will always be here for you to visit. We won't forget you, don't worry, you are always in our prayers. Your most important job at the moment is to be a big brave girl and help to make things easier for your mummy, daddy and little

Omar. Remember it is hard for them to leave their home too.

I think that when you move into your new house you will begin to settle down. I hope that it will be sorted out soon.

Sadly, I have just heard that Mr Ali, who was your grandfather's partner for many years, has just died. I have to attend the funeral tomorrow. It is in Delhi so I am going to be 'going on a journey' of my own. Aunty Naseema is coming and perhaps we will have time for some shopping as well.

Give my love to everybody,

Love,

Nani

Dear Nani,

We have moved into our new place now. It isn't a real house like yours, it is a flat and it's on the fifth floor of a block. We have to walk up and down five flights of stairs!

Mummy was a bit scared when she first saw all the stairs (you know how she hates heights). Aunty Rehanna has hung net curtains at the windows so that Mummy doesn't have to see how high up we are. I like it though, and told Aunty to leave my window. I like looking out over the city, it stretches for miles and miles. In the distance is a huge power station. Perhaps if I look hard enough I will be able to see all the way to India.

My room is quite small, there is only space for a bed and some drawers. I don't mind though, it is much better than being in Uncle's spare room with everybody else. There aren't so many arguments now because everybody is busy helping to decorate the flat. Everybody that is except Salma Apa, who is still at college, (I haven't met her yet) and Mummy, who for some strange reason spends a lot of time sitting on the sofa with her feet up drinking cups of tea. I think that Mummy is being mean

30

when poor Aunty Rehanna is working so hard, I can't understand why Mummy allows her to do so much.

Anyway, I am not helping right now either, because I am ill. I have caught a cold. I have never had anything like it before, Aunty says it is nothing to worry about but I feel dreadful. I can hardly breathe, my throat is sore and I ache all over. I get such awful headaches that I think perhaps I am dying.

I was supposed to start school this week but the doctor has told me to stay in bed for a few days. So I have not met any other children here yet. All our neighbours are old and they don't speak to us much. Tell Ayisha that I miss her. It's lonely not having anyone to play with. Sometimes I play with Omar but he just wants to play baby things like trains or bricks.

I hope that you and Aunty Naseema had a nice time in Delhi even though you went for a funeral.

Love,

Jazeera

P.S. If I do die from this cold promise me that you will look after Shebu.

Dear Jazeera,

Oh dear! What a time I have had! It has been quite an adventure. I think that perhaps I am getting too old for adventures now.

Aunty Naseema and I travelled to Delhi for Mr Ali's funeral by train. We had to set off at 6.30 in the morning. It is many years since I have travelled by train and I had quite forgotten what a crush it was. There were people and bags everywhere, it was lucky that Aunty had remembered to book our seats.

I was just settling down to have a little nap when suddenly the train stopped. You'll never guess what had happened. Two wild elephants had strayed down from the hills and were sitting on the track! Everybody shouted at them. The driver and the guard prodded them with long sticks, but the elephants just

snorted. The poor guard was nearly blown over backwards! (He said that the elephant had incredibly bad breath!) Anyway those two enormous grey hulks simply refused to budge. We had no choice but to sit and wait for them to move of their own accord. It was a full hour before they lumbered off down the track, by that time we were not only very late but also hot and cross. The air conditioning in our carriage had broken and we were sweltering. Fortunately a kind lady sitting by us had a flask of tea which she passed round so we didn't go thirsty.

By the time we eventually reached Delhi, Mr Ali's funeral was over. Aunty and I just had time to do a little shopping before we had to return. On the way back to the train station we took a bicycle rickshaw. We had only just set off when the rickshaw wheel came off and Aunty and I tumbled to the ground. Fortunately, the rickshaw had not been going fast so neither of us was hurt. All our shopping was scattered over the road, it was very embarrassing. We had plenty to say to the rickshaw wallah! By the time we had picked everything up and got another bicycle rickshaw, we almost missed the last train home. I think that after all that excitement I will stay at home from now on. I am too old for these 'journeys'.

I have just received your letter. I am sorry to hear that you are not feeling well. Make sure that you keep warm and well wrapped up. I don't think that people die from colds so don't worry. But anyway, I will look after Shebu whatever happens.

Aunty and I went to see the new Meena Praveena film, From Rags to Riches, last night. It was very good, her best film yet. Aunty was in tears at the end. I hope that you can get to see it, I know you would like it.

Love and blessings,

Nani

3. Wild Water

'Jazzy! Jazzy, let's play horses.'

'Opf . . . get off. I'm busy.'

Jazeera pushed Omar off her back. She had been crouching on the floor trying to cover her new exercise book with sticky-backed plastic. All school books that were taken home had to be protected and Jazeera had just spent half an hour covering just about everything except the books.

'Jazzy, come and buy something at my shop.'

Omar was really beginning to get on her nerves. After the kind of day that she had just had at school the last thing that she needed was to babysit. What was her mother thinking of sleeping at four in the afternoon anyway! She never used to.

'Jazzy, I'm hungry.'

Jazeera looked down at the imploring face of her little brother. He didn't have anyone of his own age to play with so it wasn't really surprising that he pestered her when she came home from school. Not that Jazeera needed any pestering today and she was about to say so when she relented. Perhaps she should make a snack, she was feeling a little peckish herself.

'All right then, Omar, you go and wash your hands and I'll see what I can find.'

Delighted, Omar scampered off into the bathroom.

Jazeera wandered into the kitchen and found some *samosas* which she warmed in the microwave. She felt like eating something hot and spicy, the food at school was very strange, a white gooey sauce over a few lumps of tasteless chicken with lumpy mashed potatoes and boiled carrots! Worst of all she had been given a knife and fork to eat it with instead of her usual spoon and she hadn't managed to use them very well. Jazeera was sure that some of the girls had noticed her struggling and had sniggered.

The *samosas* were delicious though. Perhaps she should take a packed lunch, some of the others did. She would ask her mother WHEN she decided to get up. Jazeera took another *samosa* and didn't notice that Omar was taking a long time to wash his hands, she was too wrapped up in her thoughts about her strange new school.

Absentmindedly, Jazeera took another *samosa* and another until the whole plate was cleared and still Omar hadn't appeared. Jazeera was just licking the last few crumbs of pastry from her fingers when she heard a sharp knocking at the door accompanied by loud shouts. Feeling rather frightened

Jazeera went to open the door.

Outside on the landing stood the dishevelled figure of the elderly man from the flat below. His face was red and he was waving his arms about wildly, as he shouted. Jazeera couldn't understand half of what he said as she stood bewildered in the doorway. He kept repeating something about water and Jazeera thought that perhaps he wanted a drink. She was about to go and fetch a glass from the kitchen when a small damp hand grasped her knee.

Glancing down Jazeera saw to her horror that Omar was drenched. Hurriedly she ran to the bathroom where she found the taps turned on full and Omar's game of boats cascading merrily over the edge of the sink and on to the sodden floor.

'Oh my goodness . . .'

Jazeera's mother appeared behind her and leant forward, quickly turning off the taps.

'Jazeera, whatever were you thinking

40

of? How could you let Omar do this? You were supposed to be looking after him . . .'

At this point Jazeera's mother noticed the old man who was still hopping madly up and down in the doorway jabbering on at great speed about the flooding in his flat below.

Later when her mother had calmed the old man down Jazeera was made to clear up the mess in the bathroom. It wasn't fair, she thought, Omar made all the mess and she was the one who took the blame. She hadn't played with the water so why did she have to clean it all up? Everything here was so confusing, Jazeera desperately wanted to talk to her Nani.

Oh Naniji,

I am so terribly unhappy. Today was my first day at my new school and I hated it. Everything was horrible, it wasn't a bit like Mrs Khan's class. The whole school is enormous for one thing, as big as the airport and there must be hundreds of children there. Daddy came with me and I told him that I would be all right, but really I didn't like it at all.

I am in Class 4 and my new teacher is a Man, his name is Mr Foster. Everybody in the class speaks very, very fast and I can't keep up with them. Mr Foster made me sit next to a girl called Amy, and, Nani, I can't understand her at all!

Mr Foster called me out to the front of the class and asked me to read from a reading book. I was SO embarrassed at reading to a man that I hardly said anything. Mr Foster said that perhaps it was too hard for me and he has given me a STAGE 1 reading book. The whole class was watching me and I could have

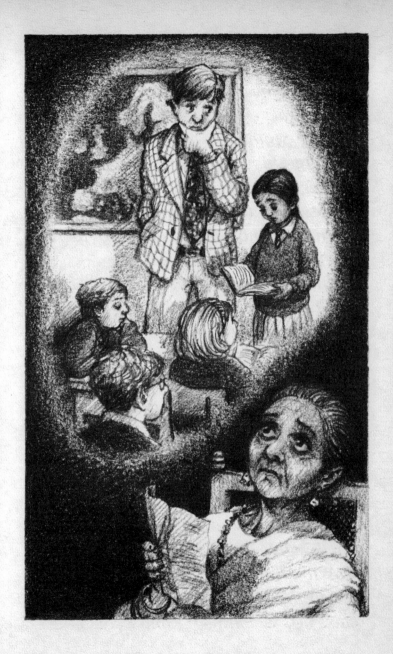

died. Now they will all think that I am stupid. What can I do?

If only everybody would slow down and speak clearly, like Mrs Khan did, then I would be all right. I tried to explain this to Mummy but she isn't feeling too well at the moment and I can't talk to Daddy because he is spending most of his time at the restaurant so I hardly see him.

On top of everything else when I was walking home from school some big children shouted names at me. They called me 'Paki', I don't know why, and lots of other things that I couldn't understand. One of them even spat at me. I didn't know what to do. I was very frightened so I ran home as fast as I could but I could hear them laughing all the way behind me. I'm scared that they might follow me again.

I'd better finish and turn the light off now.

Love,

Jazeera

My Dearest Zeera,

Now then, you must be a big brave girl. When you are at school you must speak up nice and clearly to your teacher, it doesn't matter if your teacher is a man. You must not be shy. I want you to do well at your lessons so that you can go to university and become a doctor or an engineer.

If you cannot understand Mr Foster or any of the other children then you must ask them to speak a little slower, I'm sure they won't mind. Don't worry about it, you will soon be able to speak as quickly as they do.

I want you to do well at your school work. You are going to have the chance of getting a fine education which I never had. You must do all the things with your life that I never had the chance to. You are my inspiration and my hope.

Please be careful when you are walking to school. If the big children shout at you again just ignore them. Remember you are part of an historic and noble race and you can be proud of that. It is better if you don't react to them at all, that way they will get bored with shouting at you. You must tell your teacher at school if they bother you again.

Now for my good news. We have just heard that Meena Praveena will be visiting our humble town next month. She will be filming for her next movie. Aunty and I are very excited about it and we are planning to go and watch the filming. We have never seen a film being made and, you never know, Meena may even speak to us! If I can, I will try and get her autograph for you.

Give my love to everybody and I hope that your mummy is feeling better soon.

Love,

Nani

Dear Nani,

Guess what . . . Mummy is going to have a baby. That's why she has not been feeling well lately. The doctor has said that she must not lift anything heavy so now I am helping with the shopping on Saturdays. Omar has started going to a playgroup to give Mummy some rest during the week. He loves it and brings home lots of paintings.

I did what you said, Nani, and I told Mr Foster all the words in the easy reading books. Now he has moved me up to a Stage 5 book. I asked him to speak slowly so that I could understand him and now it is much better. Mr Foster is very nice and he has arranged for me to have extra English lessons from a special teacher who comes in once a week. It is so good because she speaks Urdu and she explains things so well. Her name is Mrs Dass but she says that we can call her Dipali! What would Mrs Khan say!

By the way, Nani, I have made a new friend at school. Her name is Moni and she is very pretty. She was born here so *she doesn't speak much Urdu and we have to talk together in English which is very good for me and I am practising a lot.*

Salma Apa will be coming home from college soon. I can't wait to meet her. Mummy and Aunty Rehanna are always talking about arranging a marriage for her. I think that Aunty is busy lining up lots of boys for her to see when she gets home. I wonder if Salma Apa will like any of them.

Lots of love and kisses,

Jazeera

P.S. You must tell me all about the Meena Praveena film. You are very lucky to be able to see her.

4. Trouble Ahead

Posting the letter in the shiny red pillar box, Jazeera hooked her bag over her shoulder and set off down the street to school. It was a clear, crisp morning and Jazeera pulled her coat tightly round her to keep the warmth in. When she reached the crossing Jazeera looked around. In the distance by the next corner she caught sight of some familiar heads poking over the top of the hedge. It was the gang from the top class. Every morning they lay in wait for her and taunted her as she walked past.

Jazeera went sweaty with fear, she hated walking past those nasty children. She couldn't understand some of the things that they shouted at her but she could feel the pain from the rubber bands that they flicked. She couldn't do it any more. There had to be another way. Looking down at her watch Jazeera saw that it was already ten to nine.

Turning abruptly on her heel Jazeera ran back down the street and turned off towards the park. It was a longer route and she was forced to run all the way if she was to reach the school on time.

She didn't. Huffing and puffing Jazeera staggered up to the big school gates and bumped into the tall figure of Mr Foster who stood examining his watch. From inside the building Jazeera could hear the distant strains of singing coming from the assembly.

'Well, young lady! What do you have to say for yourself?'

Jazeera was silent.

'Come on, this is the fifth time that you have been late in two weeks. I want you to tell me exactly what is going on.'

Jazeera looked up at the stern grey eyes of her teacher. She wasn't a tell-tale and she hated being in trouble, yet she had always been brought up to tell the truth. Still struggling to catch her breath Jazeera started to cry. Mr Foster stood back just behind the gate post and folded his arms, patiently waiting for her to finish.

At that moment the gang from the top class arrived. They saw Jazeera standing by the gates but they couldn't see Mr Foster. They thought that their victim was alone.

'There's the Paki,' they cried.

'Smelly Paki!'

'GO HOME, WOG!'

Flick. One of the elastic bands that they hoarded in their pockets shot through the air and landed on Jazeera's cheek.

'Ouch!' she yelped.

The gang broke into a trot and ran through the gates straight into Mr Foster who had heard everything. He

reached out and grabbed two of the gang by the shoulder.

'What do you think you are doing?'

His face was white with anger.

'Was this the reason why you have been late, Jazeera?'

Jazeera nodded dumbly. She couldn't lie.

'Right, you lot. To the head's office.'

Everyone trooped off to the headmistress, who looked grave as she heard Mr Foster's account of what had happened.

'What have you got to say for yourselves?' asked Mrs Levin sternly.

The members of the gang stood quaking in their shoes.

'It was only a joke,' one of them eventually piped up.

'Some joke,' snorted the head. 'Let me tell you that it is not a joke that either I or the government of this country take very kindly. Do you realise that you have been breaking the law?'

'Well, my dad says that they SHOULD go home,' one of the girls piped up.

'Your father is entitled to his opinion, Josie,' said Mrs Levin. 'But I think that you'll find that Jazeera and her family are British citizens and just as entitled to live here as you or I. Now tell me, how would you like it if everyone picked on blond people and told them to go home?'

'But, miss,' said Josie, 'we're from here.'

'Not originally,' said the head. 'The blond strain came from the Viking invaders. Now how would you like it if all the dark-haired people shouted at you to go back to Scandinavia.'

Josie shut up at that.

'I can see that you children have a lot to learn about toleration and respect for other human beings.' Mrs Levin stood up. 'You will all stay behind in detention for two weeks and work on a project about life in another country, shall we say . . . India!'

The gang looked horrified.

'AND, if I hear of any further instances of your bullying you will be expelled. You may go now.'

Back in her classroom children swarmed over Jazeera wanting to know what had happened; news travelled very quickly. Everyone was pleased that the gang had been exposed and Jazeera was treated like a hero.

'I had no idea that they were picking on you as well,' said Amy. 'From now on I will call for you and we'll walk to school together. If they want to pick on you then they'll have to answer to me first.'

'Thanks, Amy,' said Jazeera laughing. It was good to have friends.

Dear Jazeera,

I am delighted with the news that I am going to have another grandchild. Tell your mummy to make sure that she gets plenty of rest and tell her to eat lots of dhal, it is very good for her.

I am so glad that the big children are not bothering you any more. You did the right thing in telling your teachers the truth.

Ayisha was in disgrace last Saturday. Do you remember Najma Shah? It was her birthday party and all the boys and girls from your old class were invited. It was a very grand party with a marquee, professional musicians and lots of clowns. When it came to the time to cut the cake all the children were told to gather round for a photograph and

Ayisha was at the front. It was a beautiful cake, shaped like a fairy castle with pink and purple icing round the edges. Or at least it WAS beautiful until Ayisha got her hands on it!

Najma said that she leant deliberately but Ayisha maintains that she was definitely pushed. Anyway, just as the photograph was being taken, Ayisha fell forwards and plonked both her hands in the middle of the cake.

Needless to say, Najma was furious and lashed out at poor Ayisha and before anyone knew what had happened a fight had started! Najma spent the rest of the party in tears and Ayisha had to be taken home. Apparently Najma has not spoken to Ayisha since. Ayisha tells me that she doesn't care but I don't expect that Ayisha will be invited to next year's birthday party!

I must go and help Aunty with the dinner now.

Love,

Nani

5. News in Brief

'. . . we do not yet have confirmation of how many people were injured in the demonstration today . . .' the smooth voice of the television announcer floated into the living room, '. . . but the Secretary of State is calling on the Indian government to take action to halt the rising tide of violence in Uttar Pradesh.'

Jazeera and her mother exchanged glances. It couldn't be. Had they heard correctly? Violence back in India and so close to their old home.

'I must call your father at the restaurant,' said Jazeera's mother with a slightly worried expression on her face. Jazeera heard her speak rapidly in Urdu down the telephone. Tiptoeing quietly so as not to wake the sleeping Omar on the sofa Jazeera made her way into her bedroom. She got out her pen and paper and frowning slightly she began to write . . .

Dear Nani,

We have just heard the news on the television about riots in India. We are all very worried about you. Is everything still OK? Please write soon and tell us that you are all right.

Salma Apa is here now. She has finished college and she will be starting a new job as a lawyer soon. Aunty and Uncle are very pleased. We are going to have a special party for her at the restaurant at the weekend. Mummy has made me a new party dress. It is red with pretty white lace and little bows on the sleeves.

Wasn't Ayisha naughty! I bet that it was one of the boys who pushed her.

She wouldn't have fallen otherwise. Mind you, Najma always gets her own way so I'm not surprised she cried. She didn't have to fight Ayisha though. If I had been there I would have stood up for Ayisha. Najma deserved to have her cake ruined if she treats her guests like that.

Guess where I went last week, Nani? Our class went to the swimming baths and I was dreading it. You have to take your clothes off in front of everybody. I was very embarrassed. When we got to the pool I was frightened of the deep water and wouldn't go in. There was so much noise of splashing and shouting that I just stood in a corner and cried.

Mrs Knight the swimming teacher was very kind and she let me sit at the side and just watch. Even though it was noisy I could see that some of the children were enjoying themselves. Mrs Knight chose some of the children who weren't very good and next week we will be going in a special pool for beginners which is not so deep.

Mummy's tummy is sticking out now and sometimes when I put my hand on it I can feel the baby kicking. Mummy is fine and she sends her love.

Take care.

Love,

Jazeera

Dear Jazeera,

Please do not worry about us. We are all fine here. There have been fights on the streets but we have stayed indoors so we have been quite safe.

There have been big arguments between the Muslim and the Hindu leaders. There was a demonstration in the town last week and things got out of hand, fighting broke out and several people were hurt. Fortunately we were all at home when it happened so we are all right. Uncle Salim was worried about his shop so he rushed into town as soon as he heard the news, but he was too late. His shop windows were smashed and some of his best bangles and

earrings had been stolen.

Uncle was very upset and blamed himself for not being there, but Aunty Naseema said that it was probably a good thing that he wasn't, otherwise he might have been seriously hurt. He had a very narrow escape.

We have a curfew which means that we cannot go out of our houses after 7pm. The curfew is a real nuisance, because on Monday Mrs Khan's daughter started to have her baby in the middle of the night. Aunty Naseema was supposed to go and help but the policemen would not let her out of the house. Fortunately, Mrs Khan had her sister staying with them so the baby was delivered safely. You can tell your mummy that she has had a beautiful baby boy.

How is your mother? You must help her around the house as much as you can, you are a big girl now. Look after Omar whenever you can to give her a rest.

Ayisha says that Najma still isn't speaking to her. Half the girls in the class have taken sides with Najma and are also not speaking to her. Ayisha thinks that they are being silly and they are only siding with Najma because she is rich. Personally, I think that Ayisha is missing you more than she will admit.

Give my love to everyone.

Nani

Dear Nani,

We are very pleased that you are all safe. The man on the television said that things have calmed down now. We are all very relieved. We have been listening to all the news reports.

Our class has been swimming every week and I am enjoying it much more now. Once you are actually in the water it is good fun. I have to hold on to a float and kick my legs. It makes me feel like a fish. Amy and Moni are very good at swimming and they are both taking their bronze medals this term.

Daddy got the new Meena Praveena film on video last week. It was very good. I wish that I could be there when she comes to visit. We don't get Indian films on the television much so we borrow them from the video shop in the High Street.

Give Shebu a special cuddle from me.
Love and kisses,
Jazeera

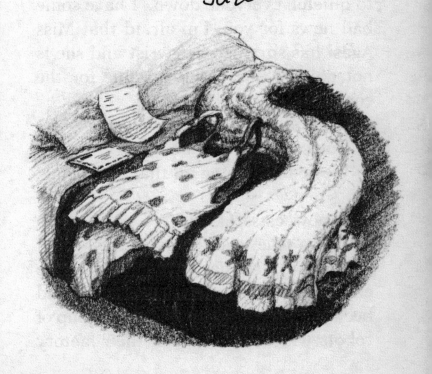

6. A Very Special Nani

'Now then, Class 4,' Mr Foster shouted to quieten everyone down. 'I have some bad news for you. I'm afraid that Miss Agasi has sprained her wrist and she is not going to be better in time for the concert.'

Everyone in the class groaned.

'But, sir, what about our story?'

'We've been doing all that practising, sir.'

'I know, class, I know.'

It was true, each class in the school was giving a special performance at the end of term concert. Jazeera's class had been rehearsing a story about a group of robots which break out of their factory and try to take over the world. They were acting out the story in dance set to some special music that Miss Agasi had written. It was lively, modern music but not too difficult if you knew how to play the piano. Jazeera had enjoyed her part as a bystander who was trying to stop the robots.

'I'm sorry, children,' Mr Foster sighed. 'If I could play the piano I would, but at the moment there isn't anybody who is free to step in and help us.'

Everyone stared silently at their desks, especially those children who were the robots and who were supposed to have worn silver robotic costumes.

'What about if I played violin instead?' piped up Brent Cooper.

The entire class groaned, they all knew what Brent Cooper's violin playing was like. Even Jazeera knew. Brent lived across the road from her and she sometimes heard him practising; it was awful. It was a good job that most of the people in her building were old and deaf!

'Well, class,' said Mr Foster. 'It looks as though we will have to think of something else to do instead. How about saying a poem . . .'

'Sir, please, sir . . .'

'Not that . . .'

'Aw, sir . . .'

Jazeera looked round at all the sad faces of her friends and in a mad moment of recklessness she raised her hand. Mr Foster looked quite surprised. 'Yes, Jazeera, what is it?'

Faltering a little at speaking in front of everybody Jazeera said, 'Sir, I can play the piano.'

Mr Foster's eyes lit up. 'Can you? This may be the answer. Well, let's see what you can do, shall we?'

He leapt up and began to clear away the piles of paintings which had been spread out to dry over the old battered upright piano that stood unused in the corner of the classroom.

For a moment Jazeera sat rooted to her seat, she hadn't intended giving a recital in front of EVERYBODY. She hadn't even done any practising since she had left India. What a stupid thing she had gone and done. Now she was going to have to embarrass herself in front of the whole class. It was only the enormous nudge from Moni sitting beside her which forced her to her feet.

Nervously, she made her way between the tables to the piano stool. Gulping she sat down and flexed her fingers. It was such a long time since she had played that she would probably make lots of mistakes. Now then, what should she play? Jazeera closed her eyes and for an instant felt as though she were back on the old green velvet stool sitting beside Nani under the cool whirring fans. Instantly Jazeeera knew what she would play. Her fingers reached out and lightly touched the smooth keys. Beautiful music poured out. It was Nani's favourite piece, 'Für Elise'.

As the gentle haunting melody reached its end Jazeera almost cried. She hadn't realised how much she had missed playing it, or the familiar white-robed figure who had so often sat beside her beating time with her wrinkled brown finger.

For a moment there was silence in the classroom as the last note faded away. Then Jazeera was jolted back to the present by thunderous applause.

'My word,' said Mr Foster grinning from ear to ear. 'We have a musical genius in Class 4.'

Jazeera lowered her eyes bashfully as the clapping and whooping continued until Mr Foster held up his hands for quiet.

'It looks, boys and girls, as though our problems are solved. We will do our music and movement after all. Where did you learn to play like that, Jazeera?'

'My Nani taught me.'

'Then you must have a very special Nani,' Mr Foster said.

It was Jazeera's turn to grin from ear to ear.

Dear Jazeera,

What a clever girl you are. I always knew that you could play the piano exceptionally well. It's all those hours of practice that you did. I wish that I could be there to hear your end of term concert. I would be so proud of you, I would probably cry, like a silly old Nani.

Last Sunday we had a blackout for three hours in the evening. It was such a nuisance, I had just sat down to do some knitting when all the lights went out. In the end we all went to bed early because it was too dark to see anything properly. The only trouble was that the fans weren't working and it was an extremely hot night. The heat was so overpowering that I had a terrible headache all the next day. We still have not been told what caused the power cut. Typical!

Aunty and Uncle have finally persuaded me to have my eyes tested. I went to see the optician, a very nice man, who fitted several lenses against my eyes and I had to read from a list of letters on the wall. The optician has made me a pair of glasses and I am amazed at how different everything looks. I had become quite accustomed to seeing everything slightly blurred and I had not realised quite how bad my eyesight had become. They make me

look like a proper old Nani now.

Aunty and I went to see Meena
Praveena last Thursday when she came
to do her filming. It was very exciting
but I have to admit that I did get very
tired. We stood for hours by the side of
the road where the filming was going to
be. We watched the film crew setting up
all their expensive cameras and
equipment. The best bit was when
Meena arrived. She was wearing a
shimmering green saree with silver
thread in it. It was stunning. She smiled
and waved at everybody and she looked
SO pretty, much better in real life than
she does in her films.

Sonny Bhatt and Ram Raj were there

too and the scene that they were filming was a quarrel between the two men over Meena. In the end Meena runs off into the crowd. Some of the extras were ill so they asked a few of us in the crowd if we would like to be in the movie. Of course we said yes! Aunty and I were chosen and so was Mrs Shah. We just had to mill around chatting and walking up and down until Meena ran between us.

Actually the filming itself got quite boring as they kept going over and over the same bit. Our legs were aching from all the standing by the time we got home. Meena was very good and Aunty and I were so proud to be in one of her films. It is going to be called Diamond Thief, *so you must watch out for it. You never know, your old Nani could yet be a star!*

God bless you all,
Love,

Nani

7. A New Arrival

Jazeera knew that something was different that morning from the very moment she awoke. It wasn't just the unfamiliar voice belting out a popular song that told her, she could sense it somehow. Stepping out of bed Jazeera followed the sounds of the lilting voice into the kitchen where she found her Aunty Rehanna stirring a pan on the cooker.

'Aunty?' Jazeera said puzzled. 'Why are you here? Where is Mummy?'

Aunty Rehanna turned her head, flashed a broad smile at her niece and without pausing in her task said, 'Your mummy has gone into hospital.'

Jazeera's stomach lurched. Her mother in hospital! What was wrong? Was she ill? Yet her aunt's song and smiles told her that everything was all right.

'Is it the baby?' Jazeera asked.

Aunty Rehanna turned and plopped a plate of fresh *parathas* on the table.

'Yes, yes it is.' Her eyes beamed with pride. 'You have got a little sister.'

'A sister!'

'Your daddy has just called me, she was born at 6 o'clock this morning. She is early but everything went well and she is fine. Now isn't that good news!'

Jazeera nodded. A sister. She hadn't really given the situation much thought before. The baby had been a bump in her mother's stomach, nothing more. Now here she was being told that she had a sister.

'Your daddy will take you and Omar to see them both this afternoon,' Aunty Rehanna continued. 'Won't that be nice?'

Jazeera nodded, unsure of what else to say.

Later that day, clutching her father's hand, Jazeera found herself walking down starched white hospital corridors. Omar bounced merrily along on the opposite side ignorant of the changes that were about to occur in his little life. Jazeera on the other hand kept repeating, 'A sister . . . A sister . . .' to herself.

Would she look like her? Jazeera wondered. Would they get on? Perhaps they would end up fighting tooth and nail over things. Would she have to share her bedroom? Brothers were OK, but a sister . . .

All these thoughts raced through Jazeera's mind as she entered the narrow ward lined with beds. Halfway down she saw her mother lying propped up against her pillows with her eyes closed. Jazeera could not remember ever seeing her mother look so sick.

Alarmed she ran over to the bedside. 'Mummy!' she cried.

Her mother opened her eyes and smiled. Everything was all right, she had only been having a rest.

Jazeera and Omar hugged their mother and said how pleased they were to see her. It was only when Omar piped up, 'Where's this baby then?' that Jazeera noticed she was missing. All the other women in the ward were cradling tiny bundles, but the space beside her mother's bed was empty. There was no crib. No baby.

'The baby was very small when she was born,' explained her mother, 'so she has to stay in a special place called an incubator. It feeds her and keeps her warm until she is big enough to do it herself.'

'Can we see her though, Mummy?' asked Omar not really understanding what his mother was talking about.

'Of course you can.'

The family made their way into another room filled with what looked like enormous fish tanks surrounded by wires and monitors. Jazeera's mother led them over to one against the far wall. Jazeera peered anxiously inside and at once her fears evaporated. How could the tiny bundle lying so helplessly on the mat possibly cause her any problems. The baby's skin was all wrinkled like an old woman's and her eyes were tightly shut. This was no threat, why she hardly had any hair!

Omar was fascinated. 'Did I go in one

of those?' he asked.

'No,' replied his father. 'You were a big bouncing baby so you did not need to. This baby came early, that's why she is so small.'

'Can I hold her?' Jazeera wanted to know. Perhaps, she decided it would be quite good fun having a real baby to play with.

'I am afraid that you can't yet, Jazeera.' Her mother pointed to some tubes. 'See those, well, they are passing food down into the baby's stomach because she is not strong enough to suck yet.'

'Urgh!' said Omar. 'Fancy eating through your NOSE!'

Everyone laughed.

'Now I must get back to the ward and get some rest. Aunty and Uncle will be coming this evening. Say goodbye to your little sister now.'

'Goodbye,' chorused Jazeera and Omar.

'I love you, little sister,' Jazeera added.

Dear Nani,

There is so much news to tell you that I hardly know where to begin . . .

Mummy has had the baby. I've got a little sister. She is called Azra. I liked Jasmine or Jade, but nobody else did. If I had two daughters that's what I'd call them. We are going to have a party in the restaurant when Mummy and the baby come home. I am really looking forward to it.

But there is something that I am looking forward to even more. I have got such exciting news for you, Nani. Salma Apa is getting married.

Aunty introduced Salma Apa to lots of boys when she came home but she didn't like any of them. Then Salma Apa brought home a boy called Kabir whom she had met at college. Aunty and Uncle liked him straight away. They have been to meet Kabir's mum and dad and they are busy making all the arrangements now. The date has been set and we are

having the engagement ceremony soon.

Everything seems to be going well for me at the moment. We had our end of term concert last week. Mummy wasn't there because she was still in hospital but Daddy and Aunty Rehanna came. Class 4 got a special mention and Mrs Levin, the headmistress, said afterwards that she was so impressed with my piano playing that she is going to try to arrange for some extra music lessons for me for next term. Isn't that wonderful!

On top of everything, yesterday I swam the whole length of the small pool. Mrs Knight said that if I keep improving like this I will soon be in the big pool with the others. Amy and Moni and I are going to go to the Leisure Centre in the holidays, they have a huge slide called a Super Chute there and a wave machine. It's fantastic.

I can't wait to see Diamond Thief. *I bet that you were the star of the show. When will it be coming out, do you know?*

See you soon,
Love,

Jazeera

Dear Jazeera,

We are all delighted about the baby and about Salma's wedding. Aunty and Uncle have decided to use their savings and come over for the wedding. They will be having a holiday and staying with you for two months.

Unfortunately I will not be coming as the air fare is very expensive and, to be quite honest with you, I don't really like the idea of flying. Anyway somebody has to stay behind and look after the house. Don't worry about me because Ayisha's mother has agreed to pop in every day to see that I am all right and to do some shopping for me. I would have liked to see you again but we will have to wait until next time.

What do you think Salma and Kabir would like as a wedding present? Do let me know how all the arrangements are going. How many guests will there be? What will you be wearing? Do you need Aunty to bring any henna for Salma's mendhi?

At the moment I am knitting a little pink jacket for the baby as I know that it can be quite cold over there and little babies should be kept warm. Aunty will bring it with her.

Shebu was a very naughty dog today. She dug up the flower beds by the side of the mango tree, all my beautiful bedding plants are ruined. Aunty saw her and chased her away. I don't think Aunty will be sorry to leave her behind!

Give my love to your Salma Apa

Love,

Nani

8. Seaside Special

Paper bags, coffee cups and cotton reels were strewn all over the kitchen table. Strips of silvery braid swung gently down and landed in soft heaps all over the littered floor.

'Stand STILL, Rehanna.'

Snip.

'Hold this pin for me.'

'Ouch, not there!'

'Shhh, you will wake Azra.'

'Omar, don't touch that. Or THAT!'

'Jazeera! Where is that girl? She's never around when you want her.'

Clutching the thin airmail letter Jazeera wandered into her bedroom intently reading her grandmother's tiny writing. Poor Nani was the one who had to stay behind. Although she knew that it wasn't possible Jazeera wished that it was Uncle Salim who wasn't coming. Despondently she perched on the edge of her bed and thought about how much she wanted to see Nani again. Life was just not fair. Hearing her mother's anxious call Jazeera headed into the kitchen.

'Jazeera, take Omar out of here, we're trying to make Aunty's suit for the wedding and he's messing up all my material.'

Jazeera's mother bent down and snatched a piece of pink satin from Omar's head just as he was about to turn himself into a ghost with it.

'Go on, you two, out of here.'

'Where shall we go, Mummy?' Jazeera said trying to catch hold of a squirming Omar.

'I don't know, but don't wake Azra whatever you do.'

DING DONG.

'Go and see who that is, will you, Jazeera?'

Outside the door stood Salma and Kabir. Omar shrieked with delight at seeing his cousin-to-be and ran full pelt into him.

'Hello, kids,' Kabir said cheerfully rubbing Omar's hair back the wrong way.

'How are things going in here?' Salma called into the kitchen.

'Umragharph,' Jazeera's mother mumbled through a mouthful of pins.

'We've decided to take a trip down to the seaside. Shall we take the children?'

Whatever Jazeera's mother said in reply was completely lost in the hubbub of delight from Jazeera and Omar.

An hour and a half later Jazeera sat in the car straining her eyes over the horizon to catch the first glimpse of the sea. Kabir had promised it was about to appear. She forgot her disappointment over Nani's news in the excitement of seeing the sea for the first time in her life.

'Look, there it is!' cried Salma.

Jazeera gazed in wonder as their little car wove through the streets and out on to the promenade. It was big, she knew that it would be big but she hadn't expected it to be quite so noisy. Gulls squawked overhead as they dipped and dived through the air, waves crashed against the shore sending up a fine white spray and little pebbles tinkled against each other as each wave receded.

Omar, whooping with delight, was behaving as though he were suspended on a piece of elastic while Salma and Kabir unpacked large bags from the car. Jazeera stood transfixed staring out over the vast expanse of moving water. A slight breeze tugged at her hair and brought with it wave after wave of fishy, salty smells. Jazeera breathed in deeply. It was fabulous and even she couldn't help running beside Omar over the crunchy pebbles and on to the patch of deep brown sand that was steadily filling up with sunbathers.

As she patted mushy wet sand into Omar's red plastic bucket and turned it out on to the castle that they were building, Jazeera realised that this was the first time since leaving India that she had felt the sun on her bare skin. It wasn't as fierce as the heat back home but the sunshine soothed her body and beside this lively sea everything felt so refreshing.

Later Jazeera stood by the water's edge and watched the waves lap backwards and forwards over her feet. It was peaceful seeing the flurry of white foam chase itself across her toes.

'Come on, Jazeera,' Salma Apa called. 'It's time to go.'

Jazeera didn't want to go. She was enjoying herself, surely it was too early to leave. She ignored the call.

'Hurry up, Jazeera,' Salma called, more urgently this time. 'We're going to the fair.'

Jazeera didn't ignore that. Up she jumped and ran over to the towels where her cousin was rubbing Omar's legs vigorously.

'The fairground, really! Where is it?'

'Over there.' Kabir pointed to the end of the promenade. Sure enough Jazeera could make out tops of the rides in the distance. She had been so wrapped up with the sea that she hadn't thought to look behind her.

Dried and dressed they made their way under the big clown's face welcoming them to the fairground. Jazeera held Salma's hand as they pushed their way between rides and people. Everything looked so bright and jolly that Jazeera didn't know which ride to go on first. In the end Omar chose the large roundabout with the gleaming horses. After that there was no stopping them; they went on the

swinging boats, the circular train (for Omar) and Kabir won a fluffy pink teddy on the hoopla stall.

As they stood munching on gigantic candyflosses Jazeera's eye caught sight of a very big ride at the back of the fairground.

'That's it,' Jazeera said tugging Kabir's sleeve. 'That's the one I want to go on.'

'We can't take Omar on the Big Dipper,' said Salma sounding quite worried.

'I don't see why not, we'll all be strapped in. Anyway, I'll hold on to him, don't worry.'

Minutes later they were being secured into their seats. Jazeera sensed a mounting tension among the passengers. They were off. The car lurched forward and began its slow relentless climb. At the peak of the track Jazeera looked out and saw the fairground spread like a picnic before her then suddenly her breath was whipped out of her mouth as the car hurtled down the track at breakneck speed. Surely they would be thrown out of their seats, but no, the car was grinding slowly upwards again. Clutching the rail in front of her for dear life Jazeera's body lifted out of its seat as they went careering down the next slope. They were going too fast, they must surely fall off. No they were tearing round a sharp bend – now they would fall out instead ... Two more

death-defying swoops and the carriage trundled back to the start.

With wobbly legs everyone climbed out.

'See, Salma,' said Kabir pointing to Omar. 'He's all right.'

Before Salma could nod in agreement Omar bent over and retched, bringing up the contents of his stomach! Fortunately none of the mess went on his clothes. Omar was very quiet for the rest of the afternoon.

'That's the last time that I take you on the Big Dipper,' joked Kabir as they drove home. But Omar was already fast asleep, the excitement of the day had worn him out. It had also worn Jazeera out but she was too exhilarated to sleep. She sat quietly in the back of the car remembering all the lovely things that had happened.

'It's not the last time that you'll take *me* though, is it?'

Kabir smiled.

'I wish that Nani could have come to

the seaside,' Jazeera sighed remembering her grandmother fondly.

'Yes, I don't think that she will have ever seen the sea,' said Salma Apa. 'But I don't think that she would like to go on the Big Dipper.'

'No,' Jazeera smiled. 'Not the Big Dipper.'

Dear Nani,

Everyone is very busy here. Mummy has to get up in the night and feed Azra when she cries. At first I used to wake up as well but now I am used to it and I just go back to sleep.

Aunty and Salma Apa come round nearly every day to see the baby and to discuss the wedding plans. They have arranged the food and the music and booked the Civic Hall. There will be about 700 people coming, I think.

Mummy is buying me a new gold and purple Salwar Kameez. *I have seen it and it looks very grand. Salma Apa says that she wants me to wear flowers in my hair and she has bought me some new gold bangles. Even Omar has got a new suit with a little bow tie to wear.*

I was so upset when I read that you weren't coming. It will be nice to see Aunty and Uncle, of course, but I wish that you were coming as well. Couldn't somebody else look after the house?

Flying is not scary at all. When we came here I forgot that I was on an aeroplane most of the time.

There is so much that I wanted to show you. We have a shopping arcade with fifty shops all under one roof and Omar and I have our own library

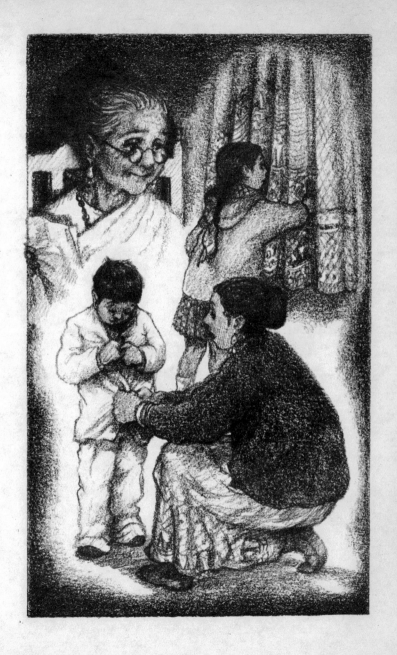

tickets. They even have books in Urdu and Hindi. But most of all I wanted to take you to the seaside. I cannot explain how wonderful it is, I know that you would enjoy it.

I will be thinking about you all through the wedding.

Love,

Jazeera

9. *More Arrivals*

From their position on the roof above the airport terminal Jazeera and her family had a clear view of the huge runways stretching out like ribbons below. They had arrived at the airport early and had gone up to the spectators' platform to watch the many aeroplanes taking off and landing while they waited.

The whole family had turned out and they made a colourful line along the barrier as they gazed up to the sky watching for one particular plane. Salma and Kabir stood shyly to one side and spoke to each other occasionally in soft whispers. Jazeera's mother and

Aunty Rehanna, with sarees flapping in the breeze, took it in turns to hold baby Azra. Omar, of course, was in his element. He rushed madly from one side of the roof to the other agog with excitement and gave anybody who would listen a running commentary on what was happening on the airstrips below.

Jazeera stood beside her father. He tended not to join in much with the

women's talk and Uncle Javed, whom he usually talked to, had agreed to be the one to stay behind at the restaurant. He was busy preparing the upstairs room for the grand celebration for the new arrivals.

Jazeera glanced down at her watch, it was exactly 2 pm. Lifting her eyes Jazeera scanned the puffy white clouds above. There was nothing there. She screwed up her eyes and looked harder.

From behind a large cloud appeared a plane and on its tail was the distinctive green and orange of Air India.

'It's here,' Jazeera cried pointing heavenwards.

With one movement her family's heads turned to the direction that she was pointing.

'Dot on time,' Jazeera's father noted with approval tapping his watch.

'Can we go and see Aunty now?' Omar shouted bouncing up and down as the huge Jumbo jet slid gracefully on to the runway, coasted to a slow crawl and then taxied smoothly to a waiting gate.

'Not yet,' Jazeera's mother explained. 'They will have to collect their luggage and then go through customs. But we can go downstairs and wait for them.'

In the arrivals lounge Jazeera found herself squashed up against the barrier amidst a great throng of people all patiently waiting for their family and friends to appear. With her forehead pressed against the upper rung of the

barrier Jazeera wished once again that Nani had been able to come. She was looking forward to seeing Aunty Naseema and Uncle Salim again, but it wasn't the same without Nani. She tried to be brave about it but inside she felt as though a heavy stone had been tied down in her stomach. Jazeera sighed to herself and stared ahead forlornly at the heavy double door.

As she watched, the doors swung open and a stream of saree-clad women, sleepy children and men pushing trolleys piled high with suitcases began to emerge. Jazeera watched the tired passengers file past her as though she were the queen inspecting her troops.

'There they are!' Jazeera's father exclaimed.

Jazeera looked and there, pushing a trolley filled with cases, was the friendly face of Uncle Salim. Beside him walked Aunty Naseema also laden with bags and a small case. Jazeera smiled at the sight of them, but what she saw next made her stand bolt upright, for following behind on ageing legs was a white-robed figure wearing tiny round gold glasses and clutching a white cardigan about her stooping shoulders.

'Nani!' yelled Jazeera wild with delight.

Before anyone could stop her Jazeera had scaled the barrier, jumped down the other side and darted off across the wide concourse and into the open arms of her grandmother.

'Oh, Zeeraji!' Nani cried. 'How I've missed you.'

For a few moments time froze as grandmother and granddaughter stood holding each other in rapt silence. Then it was over, voices greeted, faces kissed, backs were slapped and hands shaken as the rest of the family came over to greet the new arrivals.

'What do you think of this then, Jazeera?' her father asked putting his arm round his daughter and giving her a squeeze.

'It's wonderful. I thought that you weren't coming.' Jazeera looked up at Nani's smiling face.

'Neither did I,' Nani replied. 'Your daddy decided that I should come. He has been saving up and he sent me the money for the ticket just in time. We didn't tell you because we wanted it to be a surprise.'

'It is,' Jazeera agreed. 'The best surprise ever.'

With a smile on her face set to outshine the sun Jazeera danced a happy jig as her family left the arrivals lounge. Nani was here. There was so much to talk about, so many places to go, so much to do. She hardly knew where to begin . . .

Words that you may not know:

Apa	term of respect for an older sister or female cousin
Dhal	lentil dish
Henna	brightly coloured dye
-ji	term of affection and respect
Mendhi	intricate pattern painted on a bride's hand for decoration
Nani	maternal grandmother
Parathas	stuffed and lightly fried flat bread
Wallah	worker